To Kevin Muse: Thank you for inspiring this story with a photograph.

Thanks to all who have supported us: Ben Muse, Rhonda Muse, Jimmy McCullough, Sherri McCullough, James McCullough, Mary McCullough, Freedom Church, my BCM friends and my friends at Capital Directions.

Special thanks to Andrew Allen for reviewing my words and making them better.

"Let us remember that the Christmas heart is a giving heart, a wide open heart that thinks of others first."
-George Matthew Adams, The Christmas Heart

The Christmas Owl

Written by
Angela Muse

Illustrated by
Helen H. Wu

One December day a bitter wind blew steady.
And snow fell thick like Jack Frost's confetti.

A young Barred owl had fallen from his perch.
Injured and cold for safe harbor he searched.

Though his wings weren't broken, he
was too weak to fly.
He had to find shelter on this cold,
snowy night.

He slowly hopped into a jack rabbit's den.
Was the space too cramped for him to
come in?

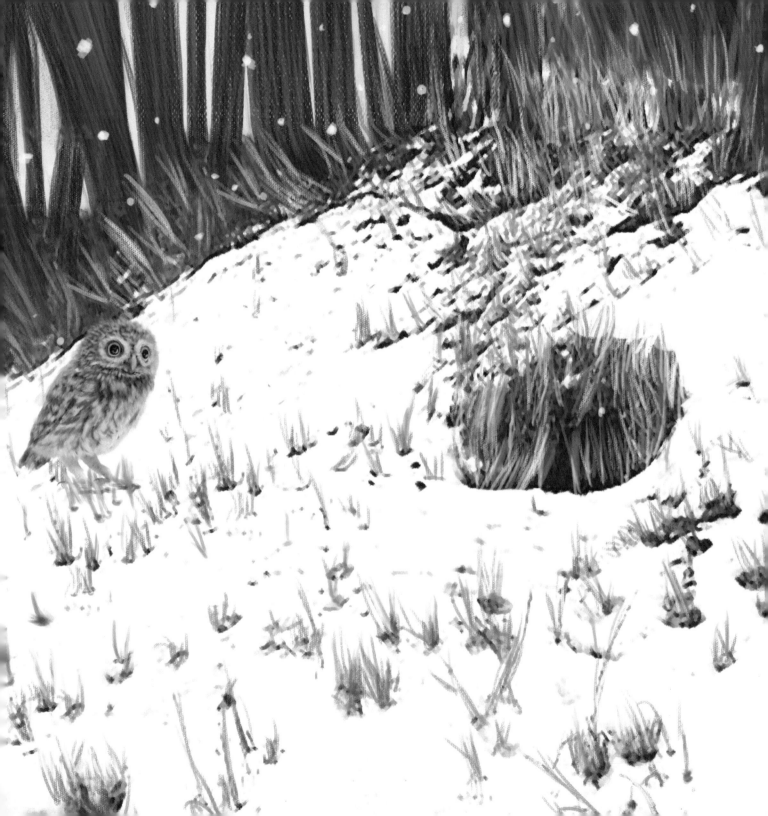

The sharp owl talons frightened the hare.
"You can't stay here; I've no room to spare."

"Please sir, just let me stay for one night.
My wings must heal before I can take flight."

"What will you eat?" asked the nervous rabbit.
"Would you share some bites of your
tasty carrots?"

"Show me this kindness and I'll return it
again."
With that, the rabbit welcomed him in.

The next day the owl was still on the mend.
He hopped up to a warm cave to lay
his weary head.

A bat approached; she seemed upset.
"You cannot stay here, I sincerely regret."

"Please miss, just let me stay for one night.
My wings must heal before I can take flight."

The bat asked the owl, "What will you eat?"
"I 'd gladly make due with some fruit
as a treat."

The bat read a book before falling asleep.
Soon she was snoring not making a peep.

The next morning the owl set out again.
Still feeling weak, still on the mend.

A red barn door was left open wide
The injured owl hopped just inside.

A small brown mouse didn't like him there.
"You can't stay here," he said with a glare.

"Please sir, just let me stay for one night.
My wings must heal before I can take flight."

"Show me this kindness and it will return."
The mouse took pity on the shivering bird.

"You can stay, but what will you eat?"
"I'll be alright with a few crumbs of
your cheese."

The mouse shared his food with the large fowl
And finally warmed up to the feathery owl.

Feeling better, but not ready to fly,
The owl encountered a duck nearby.

"Would you let me stay in your nest?"
"I don't know," said the duck, most distressed.

"Please miss, just let me stay for one night.
My wings must heal before I can take flight."

The duck made room so the owl could stay,
Trusting that soon he would be on his way.

"And what exactly will you eat?" asked
the duck.
"Some of your worms and snails from
the muck."

The very next day was Christmas Eve.
The owl was ready to fly home to his tree.

On his flight back the owl kept his word
Making brief stops to those who deserved.

Leaving a gift and a quick little note
"Thank you friend" is all that he wrote.

When the rabbit awoke on Christmas Day
He found a bundle of carrots and some
sweet smelling hay.

A stack of new books was left for the bat.
For the mouse, a block of cheese big enough
for a rat.

The duck received a perfect gift for her nest,
A warm blanket given by her feathery guest.

Each year the Christmas owl continued
with gifts.
He visited his four friends on annual trips.

Remembering the kindness when he
needed it most
And celebrating friendships with those he'd
grown close.